this is our house

Hyewon Yum

Frances Foster Books

Farrar Straus Giroux

New York

This is the house
where my grandparents arrived from far away
with just two suitcases in hand.

For my mom and dad

Farrar Straus Giroux Books for Young Readers
175 Fifth Avenue, New York 10010

Copyright © 2013 by Hyewon Yum
All rights reserved
Color separations by Bright Arts (H.K.) Ltd.
Printed in China by South China Printing Co. Ltd.,
Dongguan City, Guangdong Province
Designed by Jay Colvin
First edition, 2013
1   3   5   7   9   10   8   6   4   2

mackids.com

Library of Congress Cataloging-in-Publication Data
Yum, Hyewon.
    This is our house / Hyewon Yum. — 1st ed.
        p.   cm.
    Summary: Follows a family through seasons and generations as the house
to which their immigrant grandparents came is transformed into a home.
    ISBN 978-0-374-37487-7 (hardcover)
    [1. Dwellings—Fiction.   2. Home—Fiction.   3. Family life—Fiction.]
I. Title.

PZ7.Y89656Thm 2013
[E]—dc23
                                                                2012029684

This is the tree
that bloomed in the spring
when my mother was born.

This is the street
where she learned to walk.

These are the front steps
where my mom and her brothers played
on warm summer days.

These are the stairs
they ran down
in the morning to go to school.

This is the room
where they all slept together
on cold winter nights.

This is the kitchen
where her mother made
my mom's favorite soup.

This is the front door
my mom left through
when she went away to college.

And this is the front door
she came back through
with the boyfriend who would be my father.

This is the kitchen
where my mom makes her favorite soup
just like my grandmother.

This is the room
my mom and dad painted for me
right before I was born.

These are the stairs
that gave my mom a hard time
when she carried me.

These are the steps
where we sit in the sun
on autumn days.

This is the street
where I learned to walk,
just like my mom.

This is the tree
that bloomed again this spring.

This is our home
where my family lives.